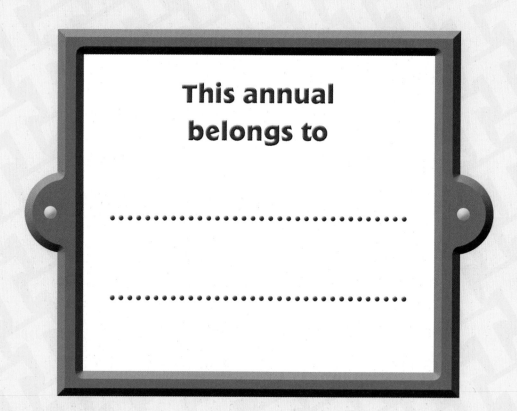

This annual belongs to

....

....

Contents

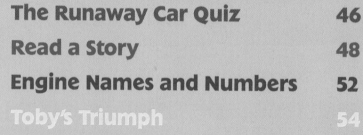

HiT entertainment

Thomas the Tank Engine & Friends™

CREATED BY BRITT ALLCROFT
Based on the Railway Series by the Reverend W Awdry
© 2008 Gullane (Thomas) LLC. A HIT Entertainment company.
Thomas the Tank Engine & Friends and Thomas & Friends are trademarks of Gullane (Thomas) Limited.
Thomas the Tank Engine & Friends and Design is Reg. U.S. Pat. & ™. Off.

EGMONT
We bring stories to life

First published in Great Britain in 2008 by Egmont UK Limited
239 Kensington High Street, London W8 6SA
ISBN 978 1 4052 3913 4
10 9 8 7 6 5 4 3 2
Printed in Italy

"Hello, I'm Thomas! I like being Really Useful, and so do all my friends. Read about our very busy year!"

Thomas and His Friends

"Hello, I'm Sir Topham Hatt, but everyone calls me The Fat Controller. Here's a song about my Really Useful engines. Will you sing it with us?"

They're two, they're four, they're six, they're eight,

Shunting trucks and hauling freight,

Red and green and brown and blue,

They're the Really Useful crew!

All with different roles to play,

Round Tidmouth Sheds or far away,

Down the hills and round the bends,

Thomas and his friends!

**"Sing the first verse of the song.
When you see a picture of an engine, sing the name."**

Thomas **1**

James **5**

 , he's the cheeky one,

 is vain but lots of fun,

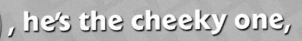 pulls the mail on time,

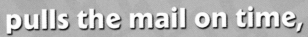 thunders down the line!

Percy **6**

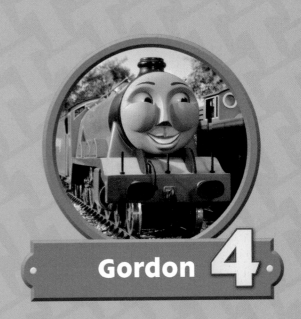

Gordon **4**

"Now join in with the song again. When you see a picture, sing the number and colour words."

They're , they're , they're , they're ,

Shunting trucks and hauling freight,

⬤ and ⬤ and ⬤ and ⬤,

They're the Really Useful crew!

All with different roles to play,

Round Tidmouth Sheds or far away,

Down the hills and round the bends,

Thomas and his friends!

"Sing the last part of the song.
When you see a picture of an engine, sing the name."

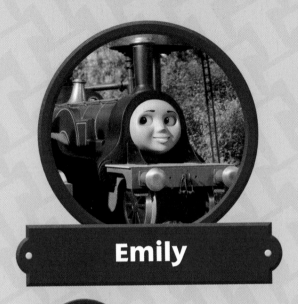

Emily

Henry **3**

 really knows her stuff,

 toots and huffs and puffs,

 wants to help and share,

 , well let's say – he's square!

Edward **2**

Toby **7**

We're Really Useful!

Mr Percival is in charge of the Narrow Gauge Railway. The engines call him The Thin Controller.

"Welcome to my Railway."

Fearless **Freddie** is very proud of his shiny brass dome.

"Here I come!"

Hard-working **Peter Sam** is always happy and cheerful.

"Do you have a job for me, Sir?"

Strong **Mighty Mac** is two engines in one – Mighty at one end and Mac at the other.

"Let's push together!"

Stubborn **Duncan** thinks he works too hard.

"Can't you ask another engine to do this job?"

Two big cranes work at Brendam Docks.

Bad-tempered **Cranky** loads and unloads ships and trains.

"Don't rush me!"

Gentle giant **Rocky** wants to be everyone's friend.

"I help the engines when they're in trouble!"

Madge and Rosie are Really Useful, too.

The Thin Controller can always rely on **Madge**, the green and white snub-nosed lorry.

"Slow and safe, that's me!"

Tomboy **Rosie** is a tank engine who has purple paintwork and lots of freckles!

"I love working with Thomas!"

Ding-a-ling!

One bright spring morning, Freddie, the old mountain engine, arrived at the Wharf to collect a new bicycle for Mr Percival, The Thin Controller.

When James steamed in with the bicycle, Freddie whistled. **"Peep! Peep! You're late, James!"**

"I came as fast as I could!" wheeshed James, crossly.

Soon, the bicycle was loaded on to Freddie's flatbed.

"The bicycle doesn't have a bell!" James huffed. "A bicycle bell is like an engine whistle. It lets everyone know you're there! You must find one right away!"

Freddie didn't know where to find a bell, but he didn't want James to know that.

"I'll find a bicycle bell!" Freddie whistled, and he puffed away.

Freddie chuffed along. "Ding-a-ling, ding-a-ling!" he sang. **"I'll find a bell with the very best ring!"**

Freddie stopped when he saw a farmer with his cows.

"Hooray!" he smiled. "A cow bell will be just as good as a bicycle bell!"

The farmer hung the cow bell on the handlebars as Mighty Mac puffed up. **DING, DONG,** the cow bell rang.

"Listen to that!" called Freddie proudly. "It's nice and loud."

But the cows didn't even look up.

"The cows are taking no notice of the bell!" scoffed Mighty Mac. "It's no use as a bicycle bell!"

Freddie chuffed off to the Top Station where he met Cuffie the Clown. He had lots of bells around his neck.

"Hooray!" said Freddie. "Cuffie's bells will be just as good for a bicycle bell!"

Cuffie hung the bells next to the cow bell as Peter Sam puffed up.

JINGLE, JANGLE, Cuffie's bells tinkled.

"Listen to that!" whistled Freddie, proudly.

But the children were watching Cuffie.

"The children are taking no notice of the bells!" puffed Peter Sam. "They're no use as a bicycle bell!"

Poor Freddie! "I'll have to go back to the Wharf and tell them all that I can't find a bell," said Freddie, sadly.

But when he got there, he saw a shiny new school bell!

"Hooray!" he whistled. "A big school bell is even better than a little bicycle bell!"

A workman put the bell on the bicycle. But it was so heavy that the bicycle toppled off the flatbed, and crashed to the ground, **DING, DONG, JINGLE, JANGLE!**

The Yard Manager was cross. "The Thin Controller is waiting for his new bicycle!" he said. "I'll have all the bells taken off, then you must deliver it to him, Freddie."

Soon after, Freddie was puffing out of the Wharf when Thomas chuffed in with a shiny foghorn. "It's an old bell that's been polished," Thomas told him. "It's as good as new."

"Now I know what to do!" cried Freddie. He had an idea.

Later on, Freddie delivered The Thin Controller's new bicycle. He had asked the Yard Manager to clean and polish the bell from Mr Percival's old bicycle and put it on his new one! **"What a good idea, Freddie!"** said The Thin Controller. He was very happy with his new bell, and rang it, **ding-a-ling!**

Ding-a-ling! Ding-a-ling! Clever Freddie found the perfect bell for The Thin Controller's new bicycle – he made the old bell as good as new!

Draw over the lines on the opposite page to copy his picture.

Now colour in your picture,
and write your name on the line.
Here are the colours you need.

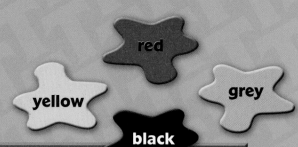

Fearless Freddie

by ....

Thomas Sets Sail

It was spring on the Island of Sodor, and a cold wind blew.

But Thomas hardly noticed the wind. He had an important job to do at Brendam Docks.

The Mayor of Sodor had a new sailing boat, and Thomas was taking it to be launched. The Mayor, The Fat Controller and Lady Hatt – and Thomas! – were going to watch the boat go into the sea for the very first time!

When Thomas got to the Docks, Gordon and James were admiring the boat.

"It's bright red, just like me!" huffed James, crossly. "I should be taking it!"

"It's big and heavy," wheeshed Gordon. "A strong engine like me should be taking it!"

Cranky the Crane put the boat on Thomas' flatbed.

"You must wait for the engineer to lower the mast," Cranky told Thomas.

But Thomas took no notice. "The mast will be no trouble for me!" he said, racing away.

The wind was strong, and the boat was heavy. But not too heavy for Thomas! **"I can do it, I can do it!"** he puffed.

Thomas felt very proud as he steamed past Emily.

"Be careful, Thomas!" she tooted. "It's very windy!"

But Thomas took no notice of her!

When Thomas puffed towards a low bridge, Rosie tooted to warn him.

"Be careful, Thomas!" she said. "The mast is too tall to go under the bridge!"

"Then I'll take another track!" huffed Thomas.

But when he did, there was trouble! **CRUNCH, CREAK!** "Oh, no!" cried Thomas. "The mast is caught in the trees."

Thomas huffed, then he chuffed, and with a mighty pull, he broke free.

But the ropes had come undone. Now Thomas had big white sails, just like a boat!

The wind blew him along, faster and faster.

The Mayor and The Fat Controller were waiting at the Harbour, as Thomas raced towards them.

"Slow down, Thomas!" boomed The Fat Controller.

But Thomas **couldn't** slow down! He whooshed past the platform, and raced away down the track.

When the wind stopped blowing, Thomas managed to stop as well. "If it blows again, I won't be able to stop at the Harbour," he said. "The boat will not be launched, and The Fat Controller will be cross!"

Thomas knew what he had to do. The crew uncoupled him from the flatbed, and he steamed off back to the Docks.

Then he brought the engineer back to the boat to roll up the sails and lower the mast.

When Thomas chuffed back to the Harbour, The Mayor and The Fat Controller were still waiting for him.

Everyone smiled as the boat was launched on the water.
Splash!

"Phew!" said Thomas. He was pleased he had not caused an accident. Next time he would listen when others told him to be careful.

Spot the Difference

When Thomas goes to Brendam Docks, he always says hello to Salty the Dockside Diesel, who shunts the trains.

1

These two pictures of Salty and Thomas look the same, but there are 5 things that are different in picture 2. Can you spot them all?

· Percy and the Left Luggage ·

Percy really loves the summer time. He's as happy as can be when the sun shines!

One day, The Fat Controller talked to Percy about the jobs he needed him to do.

"I want you to collect the holiday mail, and deliver the lights that will light up the Town Hall," he said. "Then you can take the children to their summer party."

And that wasn't all!

"Please collect Dowager Hatt's luggage from Maithwaite Station and take it to the Airport," said The Fat Controller. "You must get it there on time."

"**Yes, Sir!**" peeped Percy, puffing off as fast as he could.

Soon, Percy stopped at the junction. The left track went to Maithwaite Station, where Dowager Hatt's luggage was waiting. The Postal Depot was straight ahead.

Percy thought about which way to go. But not for very long.

"Taking the luggage is an easy job," he said. "**I'll do that later.**"

So Percy puffed straight ahead and collected the holiday mail.

He took mail to lots of stations. A wagon was uncoupled at each one, until all the deliveries were done.

When he came to the junction, Percy wondered what job to do next.

Straight ahead was Maithwaite Station and Dowager Hatt's luggage. The left track went to Brendam Docks, where the lights for the Town Hall were waiting for collection.

"Taking the luggage is an easy job," said Percy. **"I'll do that later."**

So Percy steamed off to the Docks to collect the lights. Then he took them to the Town Hall.

"Now I can take the children to the summer party!" peeped Percy. "That's the best job of all!"

Percy chuffed off as fast as he could.

He collected the children, then stopped to take on water.

While he was waiting at the water tower, The Fat Controller drove by in his car. He was taking Dowager Hatt to the Airport!

Oh, no! Percy had forgotten all about Dowager Hatt's luggage.

Her suitcases and bags were still waiting to be collected from Maithwaite Station!

"Bust my buffers!" he cried. "I must collect the luggage! But if I do that, who will take the children to the summer party? **Oh, I need some help!"**

Percy saw Edward in a siding. "Edward, will you take the children to the party for me, please?" asked Percy.

"Of course I will!" chuffed Edward, kindly.

As soon as Edward was coupled up to the children's coach, Percy rushed off to Maithwaite Station.

He buffered up to the luggage car, then he wheeshed away as fast as his wheels would carry him. He had to get to the Airport before The Fat Controller!

Percy raced along, puffing hard. **"Oh, why didn't I do this job first?"** he cried.

Percy got to the Airport and the luggage was unloaded, just as The Fat Controller's car arrived.

"I made it on time!" peeped Percy, happily.

"Well done, Percy!" said The Fat Controller.

"You are a **Very Reliable Engine!**" said Dowager Hatt.

Phew! Percy smiled and blew his whistle, **"Peep!"** He would never leave things to the last minute again!

Hurry, Percy!

Percy has to get to Maithwaite Station to collect Dowager Hatt's luggage. Can you show him the quickest way through the maze?

Now Percy has to take the luggage to the Airport before The Fat Controller gets there. Can you show him the way?

Happy Thomas

Thomas is a **happy** little engine who has a smile on his face – most of the time!

Draw a happy face on Thomas, like the one below, then colour in your picture.

Now draw more faces on Thomas. Copy these – or draw your own!

 **happy**
 **scared**
 **puzzled**
 **sad**

How is Thomas feeling in these pictures?

Thomas and the Runaway Car

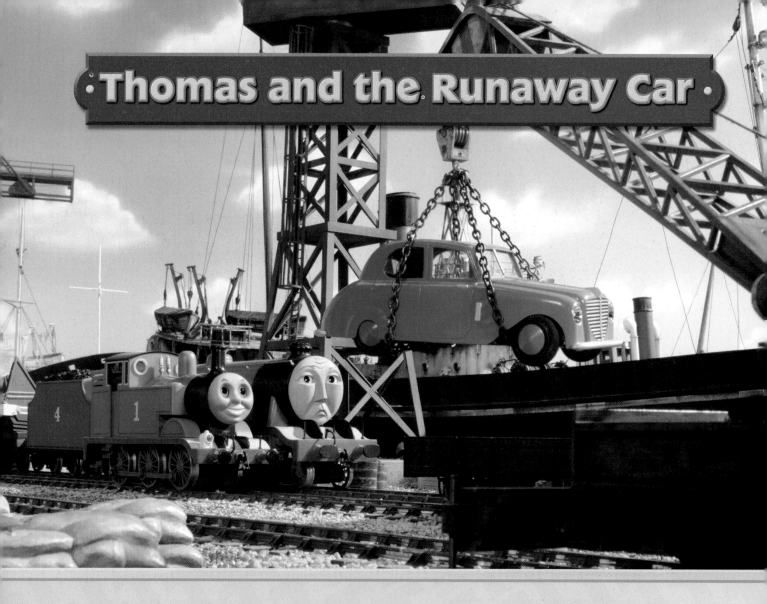

Thomas was feeling very happy.
He was at Brendam Docks to collect
The Fat Controller's new car and
take it to the Sodor Summer Show.

Thomas was so proud that he
thought his boiler would burst!
"All the engines wanted this special
job," he puffed, proudly. "But The
Fat Controller chose me!"

"Huh! He chose **me** to take the new
bandstand," huffed Gordon. "I'm ready
to go, so I'll be first at the Show."

That made Thomas cross. "I'll still get there before you!" he whistled.

"Pah!" snorted Gordon, chuffing off.

Rocky lowered The Fat Controller's new car on to a flatbed.

"Hurry up, Rocky!" said Thomas.

"I must be careful, and you must wait!" said Rocky.

But Thomas didn't want to wait!

As soon as the car was on the flatbed, he steamed off.

"Wait, Thomas!" called Rocky.

"Wait!" called the men. "We need to connect the couplings!"

But Thomas took no notice. He had a race to win!

The fastest way to the Summer Show was over Gordon's Hill. Thomas' axles tingled and his wheels trembled as he ran up the steep slope.

"Whee!" he gasped when he got to the top of the hill, then, **"Whoooaaa!"** he cried as the flatbed with the car ran away down the other side!

"Oh, no!" cried Thomas, racing after the runaway car. "Stop! Stop! Wait for me!"

The car raced along by itself until it came to works on the track. There was thick mud everywhere!

Rosie was at the washdown when she saw the car racing towards her.

"Bust my buffers!" she cried, as it covered her in mud.

"Sorry, Rosie!" tooted Thomas, as he chuffed by.

The runaway car sped towards the Junction, where Gordon was waiting with the bandstand. It raced past him then, **crash! crump!** It went off the tracks and ended up in a haystack!

"I told you I'd get to the Show first, Thomas!" said Gordon, as Thomas puffed up behind him.

Thomas huffed up to the haystack. **"Cinders and ashes!"** he cried. "I've lost the race! And now The Fat Controller's new car won't be at the Show on time! I'll have to go back to the Docks for Rocky. But I'm not strong enough to pull him on my own."

Before long, Gordon came back down the line. He had won the race and delivered the bandstand.

"Gordon," whistled Thomas, "will you please go and collect Rocky for me? I'm not strong enough."

Gordon felt sorry for Thomas. "Yes, of course I will," he said, kindly.

Gordon raced to the Docks where he collected Rocky, then steamed back as fast as he could.

This time, Thomas waited patiently as Rocky lifted The Fat Controller's car out of the haystack.

"Would you like to deliver The Fat Controller's car, Gordon?" asked Thomas. It was his way of saying thank you.

Gordon was pleased to have the most important job. "I would," he said. "Thank you, Thomas."

This time there was no race. The two friends arrived at the Summer Show together.

The Fat Controller was very pleased with his new car, and everyone clapped and cheered when they saw it.

Can you guess who cheered loudest of them all? Yes, it was Thomas. **"Hurray!"** he cried, happily!

The Runaway Car Quiz

Did you enjoy the story about Thomas and the Runaway Car? Can you answer these questions about it, and tick the right answers?

1. Who did Thomas collect a new car for?

The Thin Controller

Lady Hatt

The Fat Controller

2. What colour was the new car?

red

yellow

blue

3. Who took the new bandstand to the Sodor Summer Show?

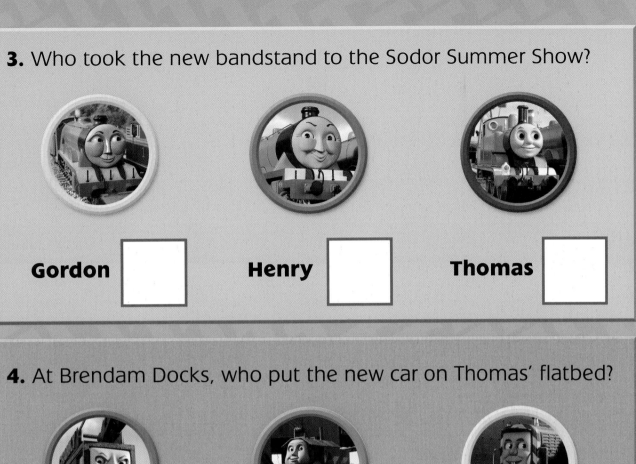

Gordon   □   **Henry**   □   **Thomas**   □

4. At Brendam Docks, who put the new car on Thomas' flatbed?

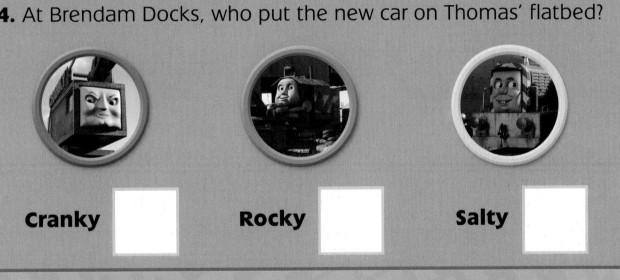

Cranky   □   **Rocky**   □   **Salty**   □

5. Which engine was covered in mud by the runaway car?

Rosie   □   **James**   □   **Emily**   □

Read a Story

Now you know what happened in the story, you can read it yourself! The little pictures will help you. When you see the pictures of Thomas and his friends, say their names.

The Fat Controller

Thomas

Gordon

Rocky

Rosie

One day,  asks  to take

his new car to the Summer Show.

 asks  to take the bandstand.

 and  are very excited.

 puts the car on the flatbed.

"Hurry, !" says . "I want

to get to the Summer Show before

!" "You must wait, ," says

. But  will not wait.

sets off before  fixes the car on

properly!  goes as fast as he can.

"I'll beat  yet!" puffs  .

At the top of a hill, the car runs away

from  ! It covers poor  in

mud, then crashes into a haystack!

 comes to help  .  brings

 who rescues the car. "  ,

do you want to take the car for

 ?" asks  . "Yes," says  .

 feels very pleased and proud.

 and  go to the Summer

Show together.  is very pleased

with his new car. is very pleased

with  and , too! "  and

, you are both Really Useful

Engines!" says . **"Peep!"** says

, happily. **"Wheesh!"** says .

Engine Names and Numbers

Thomas and his friends have numbers as well as names.
Colour in the right number for each engine. Look back through
the book if you need help!

Thomas   1 2 3 4 5 6 7

Henry   1 2 3 4 5 6 7

Toby   1 2 3 4 5 6 7

Percy

1 2 3 4 5 6 7

Gordon

1 2 3 4 5 6 7

Edward

1 2 3 4 5 6 7

James

1 2 3 4 5 6 7

ANSWERS: Thomas – 1, Henry – 3, Toby – 7, Percy – 6, Gordon – 4, Edward – 2, James – 5.

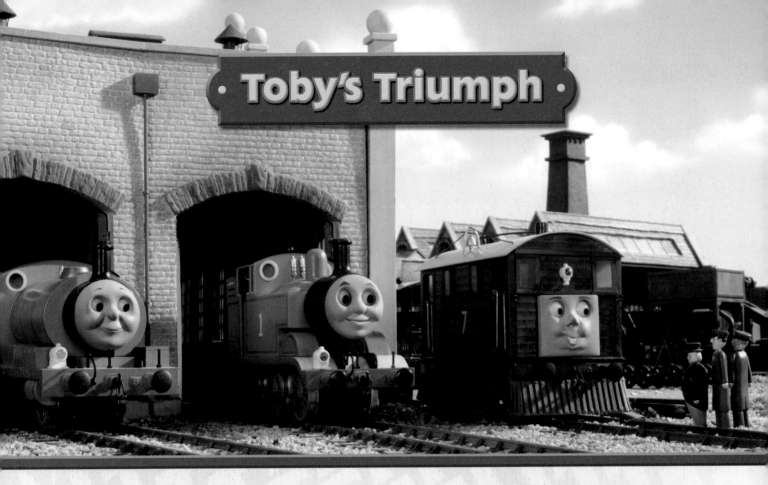

· Toby's Triumph ·

It was autumn on the Island of Sodor, and time for the Harvest Festival Picnic.

All the engines were busy, puffing around, and delivering things.

One morning, The Fat Controller went to Tidmouth Station.

"Alicia Botti, the famous singer, is coming to perform at the Harvest Picnic," he told the engines. "Toby, I need you and Henrietta to take her from the Airport to the picnic. Remember, she is a Very Special Passenger. I am relying on you to do a very good job."

"I've never taken a Very Special Passenger before," said Toby later, when he was being cleaned and polished. "I'm worried I'll make a mistake."

When he saw the extra-special tea the Refreshments Lady had made, Toby was even more worried. He didn't want to spoil it.

Later on, when Toby puffed out of Maron Station, he was so busy worrying that he forgot to slow down, and took the bend too fast.

Henrietta, his coach, rocked this way and that way, this way and that, and the tea spilled all over, **SPLOSH!**

Then Toby made another mistake. He didn't see a red signal until the very last moment, and had to screech to a stop.

Henrietta biffed into him, and the cakes and sandwiches fell off the table! **CRASH!** What a mess!

When Toby puffed under a bridge, the children all waved, but Toby didn't see them. He was too busy worrying about his Very Special Passenger.

Then Toby made another mistake! He took the wrong track and rattled down an old Branch Line! **BUMP! BUMP!** It was lumpy and bumpy, dusty and dirty, and the trees and bushes covered Toby and Henrietta with wet leaves.

Thomas puffed by, pulling his trucks. "Hello, Toby!" he said. "What happened to you?"

But Toby wasn't listening. He was still worrying about his Very Special Passenger!

Toby sped off to the Airport. He was worrying so much that he didn't notice the dip in the track and a muddy puddle until it was too late! **SPLAT! SPLOSH!**

Toby splashed through the puddle, and he and Henrietta were covered from funnel to footplate in sticky, brown mud.

When Toby and Henrietta arrived at the Airport, Alicia Botti gasped. "I cannot travel on such a dirty train!" she cried.

Toby didn't know what to do. If Alicia Botti wouldn't get into Henrietta, Toby couldn't take her to the Harvest Picnic, and the concert would be cancelled!

Alicia saw how worried and upset Toby was. "Don't worry," she said. "A good clean is what you need!"

At last, Toby stopped worrying!

Alicia got into Henrietta, and Toby steamed to the washdown, where the men got to work with buckets and brushes. **SWISH! SWASH!**

Henrietta giggled in the foamy bubbles, Alicia sang a song, and the Refreshments Lady made another extra-special tea.

Soon it was time to go, and Toby steamed along happily.

When he came to a steep bend, he wasn't worried, and he didn't make a mistake. He remembered to slow down, and puffed around the bend.

He wheeshed through Knapford Station, and when the children waved, he rang his bell. **DING! DING!**

When he got to the Picnic, everyone clapped and cheered.

Alicia was happy. So was The Fat Controller. So were the guests. And so was Toby. He wouldn't worry about taking Very Special Passengers ever again!

Messy Toby!

Toby was so busy worrying about his Very Important Passenger that he made some mistakes, didn't he? He got very messy!

Toby went down an old Branch Line, and was covered in wet leaves. Draw and colour in lots of **leaves** on Toby.

When Toby raced through a big puddle he was covered in brown mud. Draw and colour in splashes of **mud** on Toby.

Cool Truckings

In winter, a thick blanket of snow covered the whole Island of Sodor.

Madge, the snub-nosed lorry, was busy doing deliveries.

The icy roads were very slippery and slidy. But Madge didn't slip and slide. No, she was always safe and sure!

When Thomas arrived at the Transfer Yards to collect a large delivery of coal, Madge was already there, with The Thin Controller.

"Snow has blocked Duncan's tracks," The Thin Controller told them. "I need him to shunt the coal trucks from the other side of the Yard."

"I'll get him!" said Madge.

"But Duncan is very heavy," said The Thin Controller.

"Don't worry, Sir," said Madge. "I'll bring him here in no time!"

Duncan was winched on to Madge's trailer. He **was** very heavy, but Madge was sure she could pull him. She roared and revved, and slowly, **s-l-o-w-l-y**, pulled away.

Madge drove carefully, being safe and sure.

But Duncan teased her. "You always go so slowly," he said. "We'll be lucky to get to the Transfer Yards by teatime!"

"I do my jobs safely and on time," said Madge.

"But going by road will be dull," puffed Duncan. "Not fast and exciting – the way I like it!"

Suddenly, Madge turned up a narrow mountain road. "I'll show you something fast and exciting!" she said.

Madge made her wheels skid, and snow sprayed up on to the side of the road.

"Wow!" said Duncan. "Do it again!"

Madge sprayed snow all along the road, then she sprayed the trees and bushes – and even a policeman!

"Sorry!" said Madge.

Madge and Duncan were having so much fun that they forgot all about getting to the Transfer Yards, where Thomas and The Thin Controller were waiting with the coal trucks.

Madge took Duncan to the top of a hill, then raced down it. She slid around corners and skidded over bumps.

But halfway down the hill there was a very sharp turn. And the road was very icy.

"Watch out!" puffed Duncan.

"Oh, no!" gasped Madge.

She braked hard, but it was too late. She slipped and spun around, then crashed into a bank of snow! Madge and Duncan were hanging over the edge of a deep, deep valley!

"Bust my boiler!" cried Duncan.

"What am I going to do?" said Madge.

She rocked and rolled, and revved her engine very gently, and slowly, **s-l-o-w-l-y**, she reversed back on to the road.

"Phew, that was close!" said Duncan, gladly.

Madge took Duncan to the Transfer Yards. But this time she was safe and sure. She went all the way without slipping or sliding once.

Soon Duncan was back on the rails, shunting the trucks into place. He was glad to have had a lucky escape.

That night, Madge went to the Engine Sheds.

Duncan told the other engines about his trip with Madge. "The roads really are as much fun as the rails," he said.

"I'm glad you had fun!" said Madge.

And ... **just for fun!** ... Madge spun her wheels and sprayed snow over all the engines! Even Duncan!

Counting Fun

Phew! The engines are all glad to get back to the sheds after a hard day's work. They need a rest!
How many engines can you see in the picture? Count them, then trace over the correct number below.

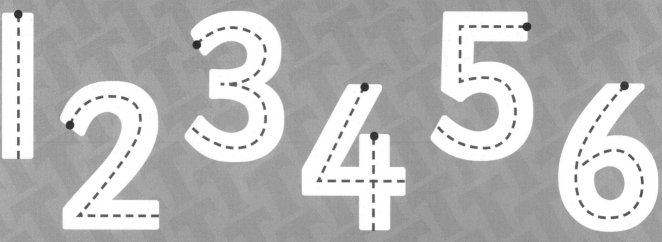